CANTERLOT HIGH STORIES

MY LITTLE PONY

EQUESTRIA GIRLS

CANTERLOT HIGH STORIES

Twilight Sparkle's Science Fair Sparks

Arden Hayes

LITTLE, BROWN AND COMPANY

New York ♞ Boston

Little, Brown and Company
Hachette Book Group
1290 Avenue of the Americas, New York, NY 10104
Visit us at LBYR.com
MLPEG.com

First Edition: June 2018

Little, Brown and Company is a division of Hachette Book Group, Inc. The Little, Brown name and logo are trademarks of Hachette Book Group, Inc.

The publisher is not responsible for websites (or their content) that are not owned by the publisher.

Library of Congress Control Number 2017963590

ISBNs: 978-0-316-47570-9 (paper over board), 978-0-316-47568-6 (ebook)

Printed in the United States of America

LSC-C

10 9 8 7 6 5 4 3 2 1

For MK

CONTENTS

GIRLS
RULE

CHAPTER
1

Signing Up or Sitting Out

As the afternoon announcements started, Twilight Sparkle leaned over and whispered to Rainbow Dash, "Blitzball practice this weekend?"

"You bet," Rainbow Dash said. "Maybe after we can all go to Sweet & Sour. I've been craving those chocolate marshmallow puffs."

"*Ohhh…*" Twilight Sparkle smiled, thinking of the candy store down the street from the school. The place had huge bins of every kind of candy you could want. Licorice, gummies, and lollipops. They hadn't been there in a while. "Or those sour huckleberry candies."

"Did someone say 'sour huckleberry candies'?" Pinkie Pie asked, leaning into the conversation. "You're not going to Sweet & Sour without me, are you?"

Miss Hibiscus, their math teacher, put her finger over her mouth to say *shhhh*. She pointed to the speaker above the chalkboard. Holly Knolls, the senior class president, was still talking about the varsity football team's win against Crystal Prep. As soon as she said they'd beat them, 0–27, the whole school erupted into cheers. Twilight Sparkle could hear people clapping in the halls.

"All right, all right," Miss Hibiscus said, waving her hands. "Quiet down."

"We can't help it!" Pistachio, a boy with bright-green hair, cried. "It just feels so good to win against them."

Twilight Sparkle thought she might feel some loyalty for her old school, but since she'd walked out of the gates of Crystal Prep she hadn't looked back. Canterlot High had been exactly what she was looking for. She'd never had a friend at Crystal Prep, unless you counted her dog, Spike. Here, she had a whole group of friends, people who cared about her and wanted her to be happy, no matter what. Every day she was learning more and more about friendship, and she was starting to feel as if it was one of the most important subjects she had ever studied.

Just then, Principal Celestia came on the loudspeaker. "Good afternoon, Canterlot High!" she said loudly. She cleared her throat, as if she was responding to the muffled cheers that still echoed through the halls. Everyone in the class fell silent.

"I have a special announcement today," she said. "As you know, our relationship with Crystal Prep has always been a bit of a rivalry."

There were more cheers and claps from students. Principal Celestia waited until the school was quiet again. "We want that to change. We want you all to root for the students of Crystal Prep, and we want them to root for you. That's why we're planning a different type of science fair this year."

"A different type of science fair?" Rainbow Dash repeated. She raised both her eyebrows.

"Instead of two separate Crystal Prep Academy and Canterlot High science fairs, there will be one *Canter-Crys* science fair. Each student from our school will be paired with a student from the…

partnering school," she said, pausing as though remembering her word choice, "and the pair will work on the project together. I encourage all of you to think seriously about participating. We'll be having a mixer with Crystal Prep next Friday afternoon. You can sign up before then on the clipboard outside the bio lab. The grand prize is an all-expenses paid trip to space camp!"

There was a shuffling sound over the microphone, then Holly Knolls's voice sounded again. "This concludes your afternoon announcements," she said cheerfully. "Have a great weekend!"

The bell rang, and Twilight Sparkle and her friends grabbed their backpacks.

The room was already buzzing with the news.

"Why would we want to work with Crystal Prep kids?" Pistachio asked his friend.

"They're so stuck up," the friend replied.

"I don't know about this…" Twilight Sparkle said, turning to Rainbow Dash and Pinkie Pie. "After what happened at the Friendship Games, I can't imagine signing up for this. Which is really sad, because I've always loved inventing and experimenting for the school science fair."

"Maybe the Games were a disaster," Rainbow Dash said. "But that amulet was an incredible invention. You have to sign up again, who cares about what happened. You could make a machine that helps kids study, or maybe you could make one that could restring my guitar for me, or—"

"Something that could come up with different party theme ideas," Pinkie Pie chimed in. "Or color schemes. Wouldn't it be great if you could invent a virtual assistant to help me with the Party Planning Committee?"

"Or a machine that could make sheet music for the Sonic Rainbooms. We could have our choice of new songs. Like, dozens a day!" Rainbow Dash added.

Pinkie Pie was excited now. "Or maybe even—"

"Wait!" Twilight Sparkle said. "I haven't

even decided if I'm going to enter yet. Signing up would mean seeing everyone from my old school. You heard what Principal Celestia said. There's going to be mixers and parties....What if I get paired with someone who is still mad at me?"

Rainbow Dash just shook her head. "What about space camp? That's the prize! Isn't it worth the risk? Who cares what a few kids from your old school think?"

But as they walked down the halls, Twilight Sparkle's stomach twisted into a knot. She could still see the faces of the terrified students when she transformed into Midnight Sparkle. She had said she wanted to transfer to Canterlot High to learn more about friendship, which was true, and part of finding good friends was being truly accepted for who you are. She'd never had that at Crystal Prep, and she was never going to have it, not after what had happened at the games. How could she face them all again, knowing that they thought she was a monster?

I care what they think.... Twilight Sparkle thought as she walked beside her friends quietly. *I don't want to care, but I do....*

CHAPTER
2

Show Your Talent

"Picture it…" Applejack said, spreading her hands in the air. "You wake up in the morning and you're feeling a wee bit nervous. Maybe you have a big test or the harvest is that week or somethin'. You look in the mirror, and it can tell by your expression that you need a little picker-upper. So it starts talking to you, telling you there's no reason to be nervous."

Rainbow Dash glanced sideways at Twilight. "It sounds...complicated. How will it read your expression?"

"I'm not sure yet," Applejack said. "But it will. That's the one thing I have to figure out."

"Well, I'm glad *someone* is entering the science fair." Rainbow Dash stared at Twilight Sparkle as she said it.

They were picnicking after school in the grass by the Wondercolt statue. Cupcakes and cookies were spread out on a blanket, as well as some candies they had left over from their weekend trip to Sweet & Sour. It had been five whole days since Principal Celestia announced the Canter-Crys science fair. Twilight Sparkle must've walked past the sign-up sheet a dozen times, but she hadn't been able to bring herself to put her name down. It seemed as if it would be better to just let the fair pass without joining.

"You're too talented not to enter," Applejack said to Twilight Sparkle.

"I just...I can't," Twilight Sparkle said. She let out a deep breath. "Can we talk about something else?"

Rainbow Dash and Applejack were quiet. Applejack looked up at the sky and started humming. "So...looks as if it might rain. Crazy weather, huh?"

"Yup, look at those clouds," Rainbow Dash tried. Neither of them were good at pretending. It almost made Twilight Sparkle laugh, how hard they were trying to change the conversation.

"I better go," Twilight said. "I have a paper due tomorrow for Mr. Kelp's class."

"Was it something we said?" Rainbow Dash asked.

"No, no," Twilight said. "I really do have work to do...."

She packed up her things and waved good-bye, but as she walked around the back of the school, she kept thinking of the sign-up sheet outside the bio lab door. Were Rainbow Dash and Applejack right? Was she being ridiculous? Was it really that big a deal to sign up, if signing up meant seeing everyone from Crystal Prep again?

She snuck in through the back door, curious. She knew Applejack was entering the fair, and Sunset Shimmer had said she might want to as well, but Twilight didn't know who else would be joining. She walked down the empty corridor, turning toward the science wing. As soon as she rounded the corner she noticed Principal Celestia standing outside the lab, looking at the list. Twilight Sparkle wanted to turn back, but it was too late. Principal Celestia had already spotted her.

"Twilight Sparkle!" she called out. "I was just thinking about you."

"Yeah...?" Twilight Sparkle said uncertainly. Coming here had been a bad idea. Why hadn't she just gone home, as she'd said she was going to?

"I've been checking this list almost every day. I keep waiting for your name to be on it." Principal Celestia smiled down at her. She was one of the kindest people Twilight had ever known. She had long wavy hair in a rainbow of pastels and huge purple eyes. Everyone at Canterlot High loved her.

"I don't think I'm going to sign up…" Twilight Sparkle said.

"Oh no?" Principal Celestia asked. "I thought maybe that was why you were here."

"No…I…" Twilight Sparkle tried to think of a lie, but she couldn't.

"Twilight," Principal Celestia started, "I know the last time you made an invention it didn't turn out the way you had hoped, and your experience at Crystal Prep was less than perfect. But you're so smart and talented. You shouldn't let anyone stop you. Besides, don't you want to go to space camp? I mean...even *I* want to go to space camp."

Twilight laughed. "No, I do. I'm just... worried that I'm going to embarrass myself again."

Principal Celestia leaned down, looking directly into Twilight's eyes. "You're scared. I get that. But you shouldn't let that stop you. You can't. And as soon as you create the next big invention or some great science fair project, no one is going to remember anything else. What do you think?"

Principal Celestia handed Twilight the

clipboard with the sign-up sheet. Twilight stared down at the names. Applejack and Sunset Shimmer were already on the list, along with two boys from Twilight Sparkle's English class. She glanced at the blank line at the bottom of the list.

"Okay...I'll give it another try," she said, adding her name.

"That's all I can ask." Principal Celestia smiled as she hung the clipboard back up.

"Thanks," Twilight said as she walked down the hall, back the way she had come. She was just about to turn the corner when Principal Celestia called out after her.

"And, Twilight?" she asked. Twilight

spun around, staring at the principal's friendly face. "I'm proud of you."

Twilight Sparkle couldn't help it. She smiled the biggest smile she had all week. Then she took off for home.

CHAPTER

3

Wish Upon a Star

Twilight Sparkle hovered in the doorway of the gym. It was Friday, and the first mixer with Crystal Prep was going on inside. There were dozens of students milling about, grabbing drinks and snacks off a table by the door. Twilight saw the two Crystal Prep girls who had been mean to her by the bus one day, when she'd accidentally cut them in line. She saw Sage, a boy who always forgot her name, even though they'd worked on two different history projects together. And then there was Principal Cinch. The small, serious woman wandered through the crowd, shooting stern looks at the Canterlot High students.

"I don't think I can do this…" said Twilight Sparkle, turning to Applejack and Sunset Shimmer, who were standing right behind her.

Principal Cinch had been one of the cruelest people Twilight had ever met. She'd used Twilight, telling her she had to join the Friendship Games and help

Crystal Prep win or she wouldn't be allowed to transfer to another school. Was being in the science fair really worth having to see her again?

"Of course you can do this," Sunset Shimmer said. "Don't worry, Twilight. We'll be right there next to you. Life is a lot easier with true friends by your side."

"You bet it is," Applejack said. She looped her arm around Twilight's elbow.

Twilight Sparkle took a deep breath as they stepped inside. All the Crystal Prep students turned and stared at her. One girl shot her friend a look, and the two laughed. Twilight felt Applejack's arm around hers, a reminder that her friends were there. Sunset Shimmer was right—it *did* make her feel better.

"Forget about them," Sunset Shimmer said, grabbing Twilight's other arm. They walked together toward the snack table. Twilight plucked a cupcake off it. Before she could take a bite, Principal Cinch was walking toward her.

"Good afternoon, Twilight Sparkle," she said. "So happy to see you...."

She said it in a way that sounded as though she wasn't happy at all. Cinch offered Twilight a tight smile and headed to the other side of the gym to talk to Melody, one of Crystal Prep's top students.

Twilight Sparkle tried to ignore it, but she noticed the Canterlot High students were staring at her, too. Flash Sentry was on the other side of the room, and he hadn't even said hi to her when she came in. A pink-haired boy by the snack table whispered something to his friend. Twilight was sure he had said something about the amulet she'd made—the one that turned her into the demon Midnight Sparkle.

"Maybe I should go..." she said, feeling her cheeks burn.

"Don't be silly!" Applejack said. She held Twilight close.

"If it helps at all," Sunset Shimmer tried, "I know how you feel. It wasn't so long ago that I was the one turning into a demon and scaring everyone in the school."

That made Twilight laugh. It was true—if anyone could understand how she felt, it was Sunset Shimmer. Twilight took a bite of her cupcake as Principal Celestia and Vice Principal Luna entered the gym.

Principal Celestia scanned the crowd. "Thank you for coming to our mixer for the Canter-Crys science fair! I'm so happy you could make it." She looked at Twilight as she said it, and offered her a warm smile. "I have the sign-up sheets from both schools, and with a little help from Vice Principal Luna, we've made our teams. Please come up and meet your partner once your name is called."

Another wave of nerves came over Twilight. She looked at the Crystal Prep students, realizing there was so much that could go wrong. What if she was paired with one of the girls who'd been mean to her outside the bus? What if she was paired with Sage and had to introduce herself all over again? She was sure this had all been a huge mistake.

Principal Celestia called off the first names: A red-haired Crystal Prep boy stepped forward was paired with Brindle, a boy from Canterlot High. Applejack ended up getting paired with a short, angry-looking girl named Lotus. Sunset Shimmer got paired with a boy with blue hair and glasses named Ember. By the time Principal Celestia got to the end of the list, Twilight was standing alone. She took a deep breath and tried to ignore her stomach doing flips.

"And, Twilight Sparkle," called out Principal Celestia, "you will be teamed up with one of Crystal Prep's brand-new students, Rising Star."

Twilight turned around, noticing a boy with long gold hair with a white streak in it. He had huge green eyes and was wearing his uniform shirt untucked, which was against the dress code. He strode up to her and smiled the cutest, dimple-filled smile. "Last but not least, huh?" he said. "I'm Rising Star."

He put out his hand and Twilight shook it, feeling her cheeks flush. All her worries about the science fair disappeared. Not only had she gotten a cute Crystal Prep student as her partner, but he was nice, too.

"Twilight Sparkle," Twilight said.

"Oh, I already know all about you."

"You do?" Twilight said, her nerves returning.

Rising Star must've noticed her expression because he immediately held up his hands. "Oh no! I mean, I've heard a lot about your accomplishments. Like how you helped Crystal Prep's debate team win three years ago. Or how you placed in the Crystal Prep science fair the last two years. I've only been at school a few months, but I've heard all about your invention that allowed a computer to read typed announcements out loud."

"Oh yeah," Twilight responded. "That *was* me."

He glanced around the room, noticing that most of the teams had gone to different parts of the gym. Some pairs were sitting on the bleachers, discussing their projects, and others were huddled on the floor.

"I know it might seem early to talk about—"

"Our project. No, of course not," Twilight said. "To be honest, I only decided the other day that I was going to sign up. So I haven't even thought of an idea yet."

Rising Star leaned in close. Twilight stared up into his green eyes, feeling her stomach flip again, but this time in a good way. "What do you think of a machine that could help set the mood for a party?" he asked. "There'd be lights and music, but it could also make kids feel happy, energetic, excited. Right now I'm calling it the Party Mood Modificator. It could turn any event into a lot of fun."

"'Party Mood Modificator,'" Twilight repeated, considering it. She liked the idea of bringing more fun to an event. Sometimes dances at Canterlot High were boring, or everyone sat down instead of dancing. There was even one dance where everyone went outside to hang out on the grass. All Pinkie Pie's work on the Planning Committee had been for nothing.

"I like that idea," she said. "Have you started on it?"

"I was thinking I could work on the music, and maybe you could work on the lights. I heard there are certain colors and patterns—"

"That can affect your mood," Twilight said, finishing his sentence. "Of course. I've read around a dozen books on it."

Rising Star pulled a notebook from his bag and showed it to her. They both plopped down on the gym floor and studied his first basic drawings of the machine. He had a bunch of ideas about how it could work. Rising Star watched Twilight nervously as she read over all the tiny notes he'd written in the margins.

"So…" he finally said, his green eyes wide. "What do you think?"

Twilight Sparkle couldn't help smiling. Rising Star was the perfect science fair partner, and nothing like the other kids at Crystal Prep. Her life there would have been so different if he'd moved just one year earlier. Maybe she wouldn't have been so lonely. Maybe they would have been friends.

"I think," she started, "I'm very happy I signed up this year."

Then she leaned in, making her own notes next to his.

CHAPTER 4

Detective Sentry on the Case

Flash Sentry sat down on the bleachers next to his science fair partner, a boy from Crystal Prep named Blaze. Blaze was already sketching out the plans for their project on how clouds make rain. He scribbled furiously in his notebook as Flash stared out into the gym. He was trying not to be obvious about it, but his gaze kept drifting to Twilight Sparkle.

He'd been too nervous to speak to her when she walked in, so he'd waited. He'd almost gone up to her when she was getting snacks, but she was standing with Sunset Shimmer and Applejack, and he was hoping to talk to her alone. He was always hoping to talk to her alone. But now she was paired up with some Crystal Prep guy, and they were smiling and laughing. It looked as if they were having the best time. Did he have the worst luck or what? How did this happen?

"Flash?" Blaze asked. "Did you hear what I said?"

"Oh no..." Flash said. "What?"

"I was asking which part of the project you want to work on."

"I'll do…whichever part you don't want to do," Flash said.

Blaze rolled his eyes, as if he were already mad he'd been paired with Flash. He pushed his glasses back up his nose and went back to work, scribbling more notes in his notebook.

The truth was, Flash didn't care about the science fair at all. He wasn't even that good at science. He'd only signed up because he heard Twilight had signed up, and he'd been hoping to impress her. She was one of the smartest girls he'd ever met, and he was constantly thinking of ways to run into her at Canterlot High. But now what was he supposed to do? How could he impress her when Rising Star was her science fair partner? That guy had cheekbones that could cut glass.

"There has to be a better way to show this in an experiment," Blaze said, more to himself than to Flash. "Something a little more novel than what the judges will be used to. We want to wow them, the wow factor, that's right...."

He started scribbling some more. Flash watched as some of the groups left the gym or parted to go home. Rising Star had his backpack slung over his shoulder. He was saying something to Twilight Sparkle, and she kept smiling and laughing. Then he waved to her as he walked out.

Flash knew he should stay and talk to Twilight or try to impress her using whatever Blaze had just said about clouds and rainfall (What had Blaze just said? He'd have to check the notebook), but he kept thinking about Rising Star. Who did this new guy think he was, anyway? He hated the idea that Twilight might like him! Flash had developed a crush on Twilight Sparkle from the moment he had met her. He hadn't come this far to let someone charming and funny and kind and comically handsome swoop in. There was something up with this Rising Star. There had to be. How could anyone be that perfect?

Flash leaned over and took the pencil out of Blaze's hand. He wrote his phone number down on the corner of the page. "I…uh…gotta go!" he said. "Just call me and let me know what I should do— we'll figure it out."

Then he slipped out the gym doors, following a few yards behind Rising Star.

CHAPTER
5

The Writing on the Chalkboard

Flash followed Rising Star out of Canter-lot High, down the street to the bus stop, on the bus, and out to a neighborhood on the other side of town. The whole time he tried to stay hidden. First, behind some trees that lined the sidewalk. Then, behind some old lady's newspaper on the bus. Now he was closing in on Rising Star's house. Rising Star had just slipped inside his front door and switched on the light in his living room.

Was Flash being a little crazy? Maybe.

Did he care? No.

He crept up to the living room window, peeking in over the windowsill. Rising Star had disappeared. The room looked normal...or normal enough for someone who was hiding something. There was a blue sofa, a wooden coffee table, a striped rug, and a television. Nothing too strange. But it was possible there was a trapdoor somewhere, or he'd pop out any second sporting some sort of weird, scary mask he liked to wear.

There had to be something seriously wrong with this guy...didn't there?

Rising Star came out of the kitchen a few minutes later with a giant bowl of popcorn and a fizzy drink. He sat down on the couch and turned on the television. Flash watched him watching television for half an hour. Then Rising Star's eyes drifted shut, and Flash watched him sleep for a whole ten minutes. Then Flash got bored and sat down by the side of the house.

Maybe he'd gotten it all wrong. Maybe Rising Star was just a normal, kind, charming, smart, and handsome guy with no big flaws. Maybe he was meant to be Twilight's science fair partner, and they'd date and be happy together, and Twilight would never see how much

Flash Sentry cared about her. Maybe he and Twilight just weren't meant to be.

Flash's heart fell. It hurt to think that he might be right, that maybe he just wasn't smart or charming enough for Twilight. What was he supposed to do, when he'd never liked anyone else as much as he liked her?

Just then he heard a door inside closing. He stood up and peered in the living room again, realizing it was empty. The bowl of popcorn was gone, and there was a dent in the couch where Rising Star had been. Flash moved around the side of the house. He was worried Rising Star might burst through the front door at any second and see him there. That was when he noticed a light on in the garage.

He took a few steps toward it, trying to stay as quiet as he could.

There were some bushes in his way, so he had to press up against the side of the house to get to the window. He stood on his tippy toes and peered in. Rising Star was in the corner of the garage, his back facing Flash. He had a giant map hung up on the wall with different rooms marked—gym, cafeteria, auditorium. It looked like a map of a school...of Canterlot High. A list beside it read: *Best Places to Use the Machine*. Below it were the words *gym, locker rooms, auditorium, cafeteria*.

What machine? Flash thought. *What is he trying to use on Canterlot High?*

Rising Star shuffled through papers on

his desk, studying them. Then he grabbed a piece of chalk and started writing on the chalkboard in front of him. There was a picture of a Crystal Prep student with arrows pointing to his ears and brain, as well as a scribbled note that said *Message Heart.* Rising Star wrote beside it: *Brainwashing most effective when the words can't be heard beneath the music. Subconscious messages must be in sync with the beat.* Then, beneath that: *Message must control the entire school.*

Flash swallowed hard. When he had started following Rising Star, Flash thought he'd find out Rising Star liked playing with toy trains or he picked his nose or some other weird thing Flash could tell Twilight's friends. But this? That Rising Star was planning to brainwash all Canterlot High to do his evil bidding? This was too much.

Flash turned to go, but he walked right into the bushes, which had all these prickly leaves that stuck to his clothes. *"Ow!"* he said as one stabbed his leg.

Rising Star spun around, hearing the commotion. Flash ducked down as fast as he could. He waited and listened hard, unsure if he'd been seen. Then he took off through the bushes and ran down the street. He never bothered to look back.

CHAPTER

6

Rising Star's Secret

Flash Sentry kept quiet all day. In gym class, when two girls next to him mentioned how cute Twilight's new science fair partner was, it took everything he had not to scream, *He's trying to brainwash all of us! He won't stop until he ruins this school!* When he bumped into Twilight in the hall, he didn't say anything about Rising Star. Instead they just made small talk about the weather. And when Miss Feathers, his biology teacher, asked him how the mixer went, he lied and said it was great.

But by the end of the day he felt terrible. How could he pretend everything was normal when it wasn't? What would happen if he didn't tell anyone, and then Rising Star struck when they least expected it? What if he ended up destroying the school? How was Flash supposed to stop him?

Flash walked down the hall after the last bell rang, knowing there was one person who could understand what he was going through. He turned and ran into Frost Glow, a girl from his history class. "Hey, Frost," he said, glancing over her shoulder as he spoke. "You haven't seen Sunset Shimmer around, have you? I need to ask her something."

"I think she and some of her friends are on the Blitzball field," Frost said.

She stood there, waiting for Flash to say something else, but he started walking away. "Thanks, Frost!" he called over his shoulder.

He was so excited he practically ran through the halls, weaving out toward the old soccer field where Twilight and her friends sometimes practiced Blitzball. When he got there Sunset Shimmer and four other girls were packing up.

They had a bag of Blitzballs and a few cones next to them. Flash ran onto the field to meet them.

"Um…hi, Flash…" Pinkie Pie said, turning around. "What's up?"

"I just wanted to talk to Sunset Shimmer," Flash said.

"Is everything okay?" Sunset Shimmer asked. Rainbow Dash, Fluttershy, and Rarity stood beside her, looking confused. "You look as if it's the end of the world."

"Well, maybe it is," Flash said, unable to hold it in any longer.

"Darling, what on earth are you talking about?" Rarity asked. "You sound a bit kooky."

"I'm not kooky; *he's kooky*!" Flash said. "I saw him—in his garage. He's planning to do something terrible to the school. He's building some sort of brainwashing machine. He's trying to control all of us to get us to do what he wants. I need your help stopping him."

"Who?" Rainbow Dash asked.

"That Crystal Prep guy!" Flash said. "Rising Star!"

Rarity blushed when she heard his name. "Really...you think? But he seems so..."

"Handsome," Flash said. "And charming and kind and smart. I know. But I'm telling you, I saw it with my own eyes—something's off with him."

"Oh no…" Pinkie Pie said. She seemed genuinely disappointed that Rising Star wasn't who she thought he was.

"Wait…will you explain?" Rainbow Dash asked.

"I was at his house yesterday," Flash admitted. "And I looked through his garage window—there's this whole map of our school, and there were all these messages about mind control. And something about wanting to brainwash everyone."

Sunset Shimmer paced back and forth. She took a deep breath, then looked at him. "I'm not even going to ask why you were at his house," she said. "Or why you were looking through his garage window. It's probably better I don't know.

But I have to admit, that does sound strange. It gives me kind of a weird feeling about him."

"And Twilight *did* say they were building a machine together," Rarity said. "She didn't tell me what kind of machine, just that it was supposed to be a secret. But do you think he—"

"Might be using her to make a brain-washing machine?" Fluttershy asked, finishing Rarity's sentence.

"This doesn't sound good..." Rainbow Dash added.

Flash shook his head. "No, it doesn't. I didn't know whether I should tell her or not. I didn't want her to think..."

He didn't want Twilight to think he was jealous of Rising Star. That's what he wanted to say, but he also couldn't admit he liked Twilight. Especially not to her friends.

"We have to warn her," Sunset Shimmer said.

"Where is she?" Flash glanced across the field, wondering if she'd already gone inside.

"She and Applejack had to meet with their science fair partners today," Fluttershy said. "I think she said she was going to the library, but I'm not sure. Maybe Applejack was going to the library, and Twilight was going to The Drip, that coffee place...."

"I think she was going to the library..." Rainbow Dash said slowly, as if she were trying to think.

"Whatever, the library! Fine!" Flash said, suddenly nervous that it might already be too late. What if Rising Star had done something horrible to Twilight Sparkle? What if she'd discovered his plan? "Let's go!"

The girls ran off toward the library with Flash right beside them.

CHAPTER 7

A Little Bit Evil

"There they are…." Sunset Shimmer peered out beyond the bookshelf. Everyone was crammed behind her.

From where they were, she could see Twilight Sparkle and Rising Star sitting at a table in the back of the library. There were papers and notebooks spread all over it. Twilight was drawing something on a piece of paper, then showing Rising Star the different parts.

"Let's go," Flash said. He hated watching Rising Star smile charmingly and laugh with Twilight, knowing how phony it all was. He was using her to make a brainwashing machine! What a creep!

"Wait!" Fluttershy said, grabbing his arm. "What, are you just going to walk up to them and tell her he's trying to take over all Canterlot High?"

"Um..." Flash said, pretending to think for a second. "Yes!"

He darted out from behind the bookshelf with all five girls trailing behind him. Twilight's eyes went wide when she saw them all walking over.

"Hi…" she said. "What's wrong?"

Flash got all the way to the table before he lost his nerve. What was he supposed to say? That he'd spied on Rising Star and saw all this strange stuff in his garage? That he'd followed him home from the science fair mixer?

Thankfully, Sunset Shimmer stepped forward.

"Twilight," she said, "we have something we need to talk to you about. It's about…um…*Blitzball*. And it's really important."

Twilight glanced back at Rising Star. "Can it wait?"

"Not even a little bit," Rainbow Dash said. "I need to know right this second. I have a very important Blitzball question...about Blitzballs."

"Okay...well, what is it?" Twilight glanced from Rainbow Dash to Sunset Shimmer, then back again.

"It can only be discussed in private!" Pinkie Pie tried.

Twilight just shrugged. Then she got up and followed them to the other end of the library. They didn't stop until they were sure Rising Star couldn't hear them.

"Darling, it's about Rising Star..." Rarity whispered. "I know he seems rather handsome and smart and kind and charming and really..." Her gaze drifted off, as if she were deep in thought.

"Perfect," Sunset Shimmer said. "But he's not."

"What do you mean?" Twilight asked. Her brows drew together in a straight line.

"He's…" Rainbow Dash tried to find the right words. "He's… *ummmm…*"

"He's an evil demon who's going to completely destroy the school!" Flash blurted out. "We have to stop him, or Canterlot High is toast!"

Twilight Sparkle took a step back. An evil demon who was going to completely destroy the school? Did Flash Sentry know who he sounded like? Or how much it hurt to hear those words again?

In the months after the Friendship Games, everyone said the same thing about her. That she was Midnight Sparkle, the evil demon. That the school was still in danger while she was a student. How many times had people suggested she couldn't be trusted? Or that it was only a matter of time before she turned into Midnight Sparkle again? Was Flash just another one of the Canterlot High kids who couldn't let go of the past? Was he suspicious of Rising Star just because they'd been paired together?

She turned away, feeling the tears well in her eyes. She had to get out of there before everyone saw her cry....

CHAPTER

8

The Proof Is in the Papers

"Twilight! He didn't mean it," Rainbow Dash called out after her.

But Twilight darted through the library, back to the table where Rising Star sat. His big green eyes stared up at her as she ran toward him. He looked so innocent...and so not like an evil demon bent on destroying Canterlot High.

"What's wrong?" he asked, as Twilight grabbed her notebook and papers off the table. She shoved them into her backpack.

"I'm sorry...something came up," she lied. "I have to go."

"But, Twilight...wait, are you okay?" He tilted his head, and she worried he saw the tears pooling in her eyes. She dabbed them away with her fingers.

"I'm fine," she said quickly, heading for the door. "I'll see you this weekend."

She took off out the back of the library to avoid Flash and her friends. It all came rushing back to her as she walked down the street. The way everyone had whispered behind her back in the months after the Friendship Games. How only her best friends would talk to her. How everyone seemed on edge whenever she was around, as if she might turn into Midnight Sparkle again at any moment.

What had Rising Star done, besides be her science fair partner? Was that what it came down to now? That anyone who got close to Twilight Sparkle was suspicious? Maybe she'd made a huge mistake. Maybe she should've gone to Everton High after all. . . .

"Twilight—stop, please," said a familiar voice.

Twilight turned back. Sunset Shimmer was running after her. When she looked around she realized she'd gone at least ten blocks. She was just a few doors down from the Sweet & Sour candy shop.

"What?" Twilight asked. She couldn't help but feel a little angry with Sunset.

"I don't think Flash meant what he said," Sunset Shimmer started.

"Of course he did," Twilight said. "Most people don't just throw around the words *evil demon.*"

Sunset Shimmer let out a deep breath. "Okay, you've got a point," she said. "It's not that he didn't mean it.... It's just he didn't mean to hurt your feelings. He's actually worried that Rising Star might be—"

"A bad influence on me? He might make me go all Midnight Sparkle again?"

"No..." Sunset Shimmer said. "He's worried Rising Star might be using you for something...something really bad."

Twilight's throat went dry. *Using her?* What did she mean?

There were a few small tables outside Sweet & Sour. Two girls were eating frozen yogurt piled high with candy. Sunset Shimmer pointed to some empty chairs, and Twilight followed her to sit down. She watched Sunset Shimmer closely as she explained.

"He was at Rising Star's house yesterday," she said. "And he saw something really weird in his garage. There was a map of Canterlot High and all these notes about brainwashing people...about controlling them."

Twilight almost laughed. Of course that's what happened. She couldn't believe she hadn't thought of it sooner.

"That's our science fair project," she said. "The Party Mood Modifier makes people want to dance."

Sunset shook her head. "It didn't sound like that. He said there was something about controlling the entire school. Using it in the gym and the locker rooms, the cafeteria…everywhere. It definitely sounded weird, and I don't think Flash would just make that up."

Twilight pulled the notebook and papers from her backpack. She sorted through them, trying to find something that could make sense of what had happened. There had to be some pages somewhere that explained what Flash had seen. It must've all been a big misunderstanding.

"Oh no..." Twilight said.

"What?" Sunset leaned over, looking at the notebook.

"I took the wrong notebook," she said. "This is Rising Star's."

They flipped through the pages, looking at all the complicated drawings. There was a map of a school that looked like Canterlot High, with X's in different areas. Then there was a picture of the music part of the machine. It was the piece Rising Star had been building on his own, and there were some notes scribbled beneath it.

"To be effective, the message must play for

at least two minutes," Twilight read. *"The longer it plays, the more lasting the effect will be. Want the message to take over the school for the entire school year, so must have at least an hour of music . . ."*

"That definitely doesn't sound like an innocent dance machine," Sunset Shimmer said. Then she turned the page, pointing to another drawing of the lighting part of the machine. It was the part that Twilight was designing. "Why are there question marks all over it? What are those scratched-out formulas? These angles and patterns?!"

"He couldn't figure out the light patterns that influence emotions," Twilight said, knowing immediately what it meant. "That must've been why he asked me to build that part. Do you think he made sure he was my partner for the science fair? It's not something just anyone could build...."

"I don't know," Sunset said, studying the drawing. "Maybe. Either way, it does look like Flash was right—he's not using it to get people to dance. And because he's a Crystal Prep kid, my bet is he's using it to manipulate our school."

"Turn students against one another," Twilight said. She pointed to a note in the margins that read, *Once the message takes hold, students won't be able to control themselves anymore. The machine will determine their feelings.*

"This isn't good..." Sunset Shimmer said.

"Well, no matter what he's up to," Twilight said, "he still doesn't have the designs to make my half of the machine. He can't do anything without it."

As soon as she said it out loud, she knew she was wrong. Her hands started shaking. She grabbed her backpack and began searching through it. She had her history textbook and her math workbook, but that was it.

"What?" Sunset Shimmer asked, her green eyes wide. "Don't tell me—"

"I left my notebook in the library," said Twilight. "He has it. He has the designs for the light patterns. Now he has everything he needs to build the machine. He could be finishing it as we speak!"

Twilight's heart sank. Not only had

Rising Star lied to her about what he wanted to do with the machine, she'd believed him. She helped him do something terrible…something that could ruin all Canterlot High. No one would forgive her when they found out she was the one who'd designed the lighting patterns for the brainwashing machine.

"We need to stop him," Sunset Shimmer said.

"I know." Twilight tried to keep her voice steady. "But how…?"

CHAPTER

9

Science Fair Sabotage

Rainbow Dash and Pinkie Pie sat cross-legged on the floor, staring up at Twilight Sparkle. "You're sure?" Rainbow Dash asked. The seven friends had called an emergency meeting at Sunset Shimmer's house. They were all crammed into her living room, sitting on the couch and the floor. Sunset had bought a whole bag of sour gummies so they could snack while they puzzled out what to do.

"The proof is right here," Sunset Shimmer said, passing her Rising Star's notebook. "It's just like Flash said: He was using Twilight to build a machine that can ruin the entire school."

Twilight cringed hearing it out loud. Even though she knew it was true, it was still hard to believe. Rising Star had seemed so sweet, so smart, and so genuine. How had she had a crush on someone who was using her? How would she be able to trust what she felt in the future?

Just then, her cell phone buzzed in

her pocket. She pulled it out to see a message from Rising Star. "Oh no…" she said. "It's him."

"What does it say?" Rarity asked. She leaned over to peek at the screen.

"Whoops!" Twilight read. *"Just realized I have your notebook. Want to meet and I'll give it back? Do you have mine?"*

Rarity pointed to the last line, the one Twilight didn't read. *"PS,"* she said. *"Hope everything is okay. You looked upset in the library…."*

"See?" Twilight Sparkle said, pointing to her phone. "Why did he have to say that? Don't be nice to me if you're just using me to make your evil brainwashing machine!"

"He doesn't want you to suspect him,"

Pinkie Pie said with a mouth full of chewy candy. She went around the back of the couch so she could see the screen, too. Rainbow Dash, Applejack, and Fluttershy squeezed in beside Twilight.

"Just pretend everything's right as rain," Applejack said. "Then we'll have the element of surprise."

"The element of surprise?" Fluttershy asked.

"Like, he won't know we're onto him," Applejack explained. "That way we can swoop in and steal his half of the machine without him ever suspecting a thang."

"You should get him to tell you where his half of the machine is," Rainbow Dash said, pointing to the phone.

Twilight stared at the keypad, unsure

what to say. She'd been keeping her half of the machine in her basement. She'd worked on it every night before she went to bed. She'd been finished with the main device for days now and was just perfecting different patterns to get everything just right. She still needed to pick out the right bulbs and color schemes. If Rising Star had worked even half as much as she had, he was definitely almost done already.

Great, I have it, Twilight typed. *I can get it to you tomorrow. Also: Make sure you're storing your half of the machine somewhere cool and dry. With my last invention I found some parts expand or contract in different temperatures. Aim for 60–70 degrees.*

Already on it! Rising Star typed back.

They have this special room in one of the Crystal Prep science labs. It's always at 68 degrees. Where do you want to meet tomorrow?

"The Crystal Prep science lab!" Rarity said. "We have to go there and get it."

"But we don't even know which lab it's in," Fluttershy said. "What if we get caught?"

"We won't," Sunset Shimmer said. "We can't."

"Where should I tell him to meet me tomorrow?" Twilight asked.

"Just make up any place," Rainbow Dash said. "You're not going to actually meet him there. As soon as we get his piece of the machine, we're going to tell everyone what he did."

Twilight took a deep breath. She didn't

like the idea of turning everyone against Rising Star, even if he had done something wrong. He'd only been in town for a few months. If they told everyone he was trying to brainwash Canterlot High, half the town would never speak to him again.

"It's kind to feel sorry for him," Fluttershy said, noticing Twilight's expression. "But Rainbow Dash's right—we need to stop him before he does something really bad."

Twilight stared down at her phone again. *By the Wondercolt statue? 4 PM?* She finally typed.

Great! Rising Star replied.

"I did it," Twilight said. Then she looked around at her friends. "Now, how are we going to sneak into Crystal Prep with no one noticing?"

"Tell us everything you know about the school," Sunset said. "There must be a way inside...."

CHAPTER 10

The Canterlot Eight

The friends stood on the edge of the woods, staring at the back of the school. Above them, the sun was just starting to go down. The Crystal Prep football team was still practicing on the nearby field, running the last of their plays. Twilight turned and studied her friends, making sure their shirts were all tucked the right way and their vests were buttoned how Principal Cinch liked. She reached over and straightened Pinkie Pie's tie.

"Do you think anyone will notice we're not really Crystal Prep students?" Applejack asked. She straightened herself up and narrowed her eyes, making the meanest face she could.

"Not if you keep making that expression," Twilight said. "You'll fit in perfectly."

After they'd left Sunset Shimmer's, they'd gone to Twilight's house to dig through her closet. She hadn't given away her old Crystal Prep uniforms yet. She still had three that were in perfect condition, and two that didn't fit anymore. Then there were two more that had ripped seams and buttons that were falling off. She was supposed to throw them away, but she'd never gotten around to it.

Now Pinkie Pie and Rainbow Dash looked the most rumpled out of their crew, and Sunset's outfit was so tight it looked as if her vest might burst. But Twilight hoped they'd pass for real Crystal Prep students, if only until they got the machine and got out of there. Hopefully no one would be looking at them too closely....

"Now, let's stick to the plan," Twilight said. "There are three science labs, all right next to one another. I don't know which room Rising Star was talking about—I'd bet it's in one of the lab's storage closets for safekeeping. Let's split up, check each lab, and meet back in the far stairwell."

"You're sure the door will be open?" Pinkie Pie asked. She pointed to the school's back door. It was one of the only entrances that was unlocked after hours. Students used it when they forgot something in their locker.

"It's always open," Twilight Sparkle said. "But we need to keep a lookout for Mr. Crimson, the janitor. He's one of the only people in the school at this hour."

"Yeah…" Fluttershy said. "And we need to watch out for Rising Star. What if he comes back to work on the machine?"

"Let's hope that doesn't happen," said Sunset Shimmer. "Ready?" She looked to Fluttershy and Rarity, who'd agreed to search the first lab with her. Twilight would go with Pinkie Pie, and Rainbow Dash would search the last lab with Apple-jack. Fluttershy and Rarity nodded, and the three took off toward the school, disappearing through the back door.

"Are you sure not bringing Flash was a good idea?" Pinkie Pie quietly asked no one in particular. "He *was* the one who told us about Rising Star."

Rainbow Dash shook her head. "It's fine. We told him we were doing this. He doesn't need to be here, especially not after what he said...."

She didn't finish the sentence, but

Twilight knew what she meant. She was talking about what he had said in the library, the thing that had hurt Twilight's feelings. Maybe Flash didn't mean to offend her, but it still stung.

"Okay, we're up," Applejack said, glancing at her watch. She and Rainbow Dash were heading inside two minutes after the first group, so as not to draw too much attention. "Second room on the right. Wish us luck."

They sprinted off toward the school. Only Twilight and Pinkie Pie were left.

"I wonder if they found anything yet…" Pinkie Pie said.

"I think they would have come out already," Twilight said, but she couldn't be sure. What if the machine wasn't where

Rising Star said it was? What if he was already onto them?

Twilight checked her watch. There were only a few seconds left. She inspected Pinkie Pie's outfit one last time, but it was hopeless. Two of the buttons on her vest were coming off, and her uniform skirt was wrinkled because it was the one they'd found at the bottom of Twilight's closet. Still, if someone was looking from far enough away, she'd seem like just another Crystal Prep student.

"Follow me," Twilight said as soon as the two minutes were up. They walked calmly across the parking lot and slipped in through the back door. The halls were eerily quiet. The science lab they were checking was the fourth one on the left.

It was the same room where Twilight's bio class had been the year before. They peered through the window of the door, making sure no one was inside.

"Where do you think it would be?" Pinkie Pie asked. She went across the room and opened a door on the far wall, but it was just a closet. The shelves were filled with beakers and test tubes.

"I don't know..." Twilight said. There was another door behind the teacher's desk, but it was locked. "Do you think we need a key?"

Just then a familiar voice echoed down the hall. "Found it! Over here, y'all!"

Twilight and Pinkie Pie sprinted out of the classroom. Sunset Shimmer, Fluttershy, and Rarity were already in the hall. They peered into different classrooms, trying to remember where Rainbow Dash and Applejack were.

Applejack came out of a door near the stairwell and waved. "Here!" she whispered as loud as she could. "This way."

They filed into the science lab, which was dark. Long black lab tables filled the room, with four stools pulled up to each. Rainbow Dash stuck her head out of a closet in the back and waved. All seven girls piled inside.

The closet was long and narrow, with another door at the end of it.

"At first we just came in here," Rainbow Dash explained, "and we didn't see anything. We were about to leave when we noticed this other door."

She pushed inside. There were a few short refrigerators and a table covered in half-finished science experiments. There were dozens of trays of mold that someone had been working on and a glass tray where someone was growing their own crystals. In the middle, next to a project on bases and acids, was Rising Star's half of the machine.

"That's it!" Twilight said, staring at the box. It had two speakers on either side of it, and a device in the center that played music to hide the spoken messages. It looked exactly as it did in Rising Star's drawings.

"Should we...destroy it?" asked Rainbow Dash, picking it up.

Suddenly, a boy's voice split the air. "Why would you do that?"

Twilight's stomach dropped. The friends all turned around. There, standing in the middle of the science lab, was Rising Star. His arms were crossed over his chest as he stared at them.

He did not look happy.

CHAPTER
11

A Message for Crystal Prep

"What are you doing?" Rising Star said, walking toward them. "Why would you bring everyone here, Twilight? Why are you all dressed like that?"

The friends looked around the closet. There was no escape in sight. As Rising

Star got closer and closer to the door, Rainbow Dash grabbed Twilight's hand and squeezed. They'd been caught breaking into Crystal Prep, in disguise, to steal Rising Star's project. There was no turning back now....

"We didn't..." Twilight tried. But what was she supposed to say? Was there an evil glint in Rising Star's eye, or was she just imagining it?

"Stop!" Sunset Shimmer called out. She stepped forward and held up her hand. "Don't go any further! We know you were trying to destroy our school."

"What did you just say?" Rising Star snapped back. He took another step forward, and then they heard footsteps. Before they knew what was happening, a figure came running toward Rising Star and tackled him. The two wrestled on the floor.

"Flash!" Twilight said, realizing it was him. Even after everything that had happened, he came to make sure they were okay. He was still Twilight's friend, no matter what.

The girls surrounded them. Finally, when Flash was sure he had Rising Star pinned down, he looked up. "I told you! He's out to ruin Canterlot High!" Flash said.

"You're crazy!" Rising Star said. He squirmed underneath Flash, but he couldn't break free. "What are you even talking about?"

Twilight darted back into the closet,

grabbing Rising Star's half of the Party Mood Modificator. She brought it out for everyone to see. "This is what we're talking about," she said as she hit the button on the top of the device. A fun, upbeat song filled the air. Twilight could hear the whisper of something underneath it.

"You knew all about that," Rising Star said. He looked genuinely confused. "We were working on that project together."

"No," Twilight corrected. "*I* was working on a machine that would put kids at Canterlot High in the mood to dance at parties. *You* were working on something that would brainwash everyone and turn the entire school against each other. We saw the plans in your notebook!"

"Oh yeah?" Rising Star said. "If you're

so certain, then why don't you listen to the messages? Switch that button to the right."

After examining the machine closely to ensure it wasn't a trap, Twilight slid the button on the machine to the side. The music cut out, and Rising Star's voice was the only thing left. He was speaking softly and slowly, repeating the same message over and over.

"Kindness is a virtue," his voice said. *"Be a friend to everyone. Offer invitations freely, and let anyone join your group. Kindness is a virtue."*

There was a pause for a few seconds, then the same message started again, repeating two more times before Twilight finally shut it off. Now she was really confused. Why would Rising Star record a message like that? What did he have to gain if everyone at Canterlot High was kind to each other? Wasn't friendship already important at their school?

"I don't get it…" Rainbow Dash said. "Why would you record that?"

"But I saw you," Flash said, pointing a finger in his face. "You have that map of Canterlot High in your garage, and you wrote all these crazy things about brainwashing us and playing your weird messages all over our school. You were going to play that in the locker rooms!"

"It wasn't a map of Canterlot High," Rising Star said. "It was a map of *Crystal Prep*."

Rising Star tried to squirm free. Flash

was sitting on his chest as if he were a sofa. Rising Star's hands were pinned behind his back.

"Well, *umm...*" Sunset Shimmer said. "Maybe you should let him speak. If he tries anything, there are enough of us here that he won't get far."

Flash didn't look convinced, but he climbed off Rising Star anyway. Rising Star sat up and brushed himself off. He stared up at Twilight with his big green eyes. She'd never seen him look so sad.

"Flash is right," he said. "I wasn't completely honest with you."

"I knew it!" Flash said, throwing up his hands in victory. "I told you! *Evil demon in the house!*"

"Hush now! Let him speak, Flash,"

Rarity said. "He doesn't seem like an evil demon to me...."

Rising Star glanced down at his feet. "You see, the machine was never supposed to make people dance. It was supposed to make people nicer. When I got to Crystal Prep I had all these hopes about what it would be like here. How I'd meet all these great, cool friends and join all these clubs and stuff. And none of that happened."

"Because everyone there is just so"—Twilight looked for the right word—"unfriendly."

"Yeah," Rising Star said. "Exactly. You understand."

Twilight did. She hadn't made a single friend at Crystal Prep. Everyone acted too cool for her or too busy. When she walked down the hallways she felt invisible. Kids would bump into her, not say hi, and some would even talk behind her back. Could she really blame Rising Star for wanting Crystal Prep to be a kinder place? Wouldn't she have done anything she could to make life better there?

"But you used me..." she said softly. "And you lied...."

"I didn't plan to," Rising Star tried. "I really didn't—it wasn't as if I had this horrible thing I set out to do. I knew you'd had all the same problems with Crystal Prep that I did. So when I signed up for the science fair, I made sure I was paired up with you. Vice Principal Luna left the clipboard on one of the tables in the gym before the names were read off. And I switched my name so it was next to yours. I knew you'd be able to design the light patterns to get the machine to work. And I really did think you'd want to help me make Crystal Prep a better place...."

"So what changed?" Pinkie Pie asked. "Why didn't you just tell Twilight what you were working on?"

"I met her," Rising Star said, blushing. "That's what changed. And you were really kind and friendly and...you seemed really honest. As soon as I started talking to you I knew you would think it was wrong to brainwash all Crystal Prep into being nicer. I knew you wouldn't agree to it. I mean, I could barely even say it out loud. So I just kept pretending it was a dance machine...."

"You lied to me," Twilight said again. It was hard to even look at Rising Star now. She couldn't believe he was the same person she'd met the week before. Now he wasn't charming or kind or smart or handsome.... He was just someone who'd lied to her.

"I'm sorry," Rising Star tried. "I really am. If I could go back and do it differently, I would."

Twilight's friends stood around Rising Star, as if they were still afraid he might do something crazy. Instead he just sat there with his head in his hands. His cheeks were red. For a second, Twilight wondered if he was going to cry.

"Let's try to put this behind us," she said, taking a deep breath. "I don't like what happened, but I don't want to be mad at you forever. It's not easy going to Crystal Prep. I know that better than anyone."

Flash kept glancing around the room, trying to make eye contact with Twilight and her friends. "Um…can someone please acknowledge that I was right?" he asked. "Anyone?"

"You were only *kind of* right," Sunset Shimmer said, smirking. "But thanks for watching out for us."

"Yeah," Twilight agreed. "Thank you, Flash. I'm glad we can still count on you."

He stood, propping himself up on

one of the lab stools. He looked a little embarrassed. But he nodded and smiled.

Flash had been one of the first people Twilight had met at Canterlot High. She'd always considered him a friend, even after everything that had happened with the Friendship Games. Maybe even more than a friend.

No matter what had happened between them, it meant a lot that he'd come here to watch out for her, even when she wasn't actually talking to him. That he wanted to make sure Rising Star didn't do anything scary and weird. That he cared.

"So that's it?" Rising Star asked. He looked at the machine in Twilight's hands. "We're just going to throw away all the work we did? I understand if you don't want to help me anymore, but I still think we could make something really cool for the science fair...."

Twilight stared down at the music part of the machine. "No, we have to enter something," she said. "Even if we don't have a lot of time."

"I've barely started my project," Sunset Shimmer said. "We've been so busy figuring out what this machine was for. And now the fair is only three days away."

"Me too..." Applejack said. "I've only met with my partner once. We haven't even decided what we're doing our project on!"

"That's okay," Twilight said. "I have a plan...."

CHAPTER

12

Get Up and Dance

"Could these work?" Flash asked, spreading out the bulbs on the table. There were seven different shades of red.

"We'll try it," Twilight Sparkle said, plucking out a red in the middle. It was somewhere between crimson and fuchsia.

Based on all her research, she'd discovered that red light patterns had some of the most hypnotic qualities. But finding the perfect shade of red was the trick.

She screwed the bulb into her part of the machine and walked over to Pinkie Pie. She was sitting next to Rarity, waiting for this exact moment. They both put their hands in their laps and sat up straight in their chairs.

"I'm ready to be hypnotized!" Pinkie Pie said.

"Well it won't work until we put it together with Rising Star's device," Twilight explained. "But you have to tell me if you notice anything weird, anything at all."

"Like what?" Rarity asked.

"Any weird feelings, like if you're suddenly tired or something."

Twilight held the box up in front of them and switched on the light. She'd designed the red light pattern to go in circles, while a yellow light shone through behind it. She covered it with her hand so it only shone in Rarity and Pinkie Pie's direction.

"Perhaps I'm too sophisticated for this. I don't I feel anything…" Rarity said. "Maybe? But then again, maybe… maybe…"

She didn't finish her thought. Instead, she started bobbing her head a little, as if she wanted to get up and dance. Pinkie Pie was affected just as much. She didn't say anything, but her shoulders started to shimmy just the tiniest bit.

"It's working!" Twilight called out behind her. Rising Star rushed over to see.

"Wow, it really is," he said. "These light patterns are genius. I can't fight the beat!"

His garage was packed with people. The Rainbooms had set up their equipment in one corner and were about to record some original music for the device. Applejack decided to leave her science fair partner, Lotus, to do her own thing (they hadn't been getting along anyway), and Sunset Shimmer brought her partner, Ember, into the group. She gave him the task of recording the dance messages. The short, quiet

Crystal Prep student sat outside with a microphone. Even Flash and Blaze had put their project on hold to help out with the Party Mood Modificator.

"Will you shut that thing off for a sec?" Applejack called out from across the room. She was tuning her bass guitar. "How am I supposed to jam this song out if I can't resist tapping my foot?"

"Okay, okay…" Twilight switched the red light off.

"I did feel weird…" Rarity said. "As if I might—"

"Get up and dance at any moment?" Rising Star asked.

"Yeah. Whatever you did, it's powerful stuff," Rarity said, narrowing her eyes at Rising Star. "Glad it's in the right hands."

As they'd worked on the machine over the last few days, Twilight noticed her friends still didn't totally trust Rising Star. Rainbow Dash still made little comments about how he had lied to Twilight, and Flash was still looking over his shoulder every time he worked on the machine. But for Twilight, it was easier to forgive him and move forward. Hadn't she been in the same spot a few months before? Hadn't working on the amulet gotten a little out of control? Where would she be if her friends hadn't forgiven her after the Friendship Games?

Everyone deserves a second chance, Twilight thought. *Isn't that the kind thing to do?*

"Are you ready to do this?" Rainbow Dash asked. "Let's get through the song and record our best take." She was already holding her electric guitar. Applejack was on the bass, and Flutter-shy was on the tambourine. Rarity and Pinkie Pie got up and took their places. Rarity grabbed her keytar, and Pinkie Pie sat down behind the drums. Sunset Shimmer was waiting for Twilight, an empty mic beside her.

Twilight got into her place behind the mic. Flash, Rising Star, and the two other Crystal Prep students came into the garage and pulled up chairs to watch. Rainbow Dash counted them off and then the whole space filled with music.

"Any party's not complete, until you rule the beat," Sunset Shimmer sang.

"So throw your hands up in the air, shake

your hips like you don't care," Twilight Sparkle added, her voice clear as a bell.

"Ahem, please wait!" Fluttershy interrupted. "Stop."

Slowly all the Rainbooms went quiet. Rarity let her keytar fall to her side.

"What's wrong?" Applejack asked. She covered the bass strings with her hand to stop the chord. "I thought it sounded good."

"It did," Fluttershy said. "But wouldn't it sound better with a few more backup singers? The Canter-Crys science fair was supposed to be a chance for Crystal Prep and Canterlot High to come together. It was supposed to be about teamwork. What better way to show that than to sing this song together?"

Ember looked panicked. His small purple eyes went wide behind his glasses. "You want *me* to *sing*?"

"All of you," Fluttershy said. She picked up her extra tambourine and gave it to Blaze. "Or play this with me, whatever brings you joy. The more the merrier."

Twilight grabbed some of the sheet music off the stand in front of her. It had all the lyrics to the song written beneath the notes. She passed it to Rising Star and Flash.

"Here—you guys can read along," she said. "You, too, Rising Star."

They huddled beside her and Sunset Shimmer, staring at the sheet music in their hands. Twilight took a few minutes to explain the harder parts of the song to them, singing and then letting them repeat what she sang. They practiced the chorus a few times until Blaze got all the complicated notes right. After a while they were finally ready. Rainbow Dash counted them off again and the first notes sounded in the air.

"*Any party's not complete, until you rule the beat,*" Twilight and Sunset Shimmer sang together.

"*So throw your hands up in the air, shake your hips like you don't care,*" they all belted out. "*We're gonna get down tonight. Feelin' the groove, all right. We're gonna get up and dance! You gotta get up and dance!*"

Rarity jumped in with an incredible keytar solo. Her fingers moved up and down the keys, playing a quick, fun melody.

Twilight couldn't help it. She started tapping her foot to the music. Sunset Shimmer loved the song just as much as she did. She shimmied her shoulders and threw one hand in the air.

"Rock out, let your hair down," Sunset Shimmer sang.

"We're gonna let loose and rule this toooo-*own!"* Twilight and Flash chimed in.

"We're gonna get up and dance!" the group all sang together. *"We gotta get up and dance!"*

Pinkie Pie brought in a fun bass line with the drums, ending it all with two rocking cymbal crashes. They practiced the song three more times until they got it just right. Each time it got a little better, until they finally were able to record it.

Rising Star hit the STOP button on his computer, capturing the last few seconds of the song. Now that they'd finished, everyone was smiling and laughing.

"That was way more fun than I thought it would be," Rising Star said.

"If we keep it up, we're not even going to need that machine," Applejack said. "Just hearing that song makes me want to move and groove."

"But think of everyone at Canterlot High and Crystal Prep," Twilight said. "The real test will be if we can make Principal Cinch dance. Or Mr. Spruce, that super-serious English teacher. The point of the machine is to make everyone get on the dance floor together, no matter how shy or scared they are. Even the people who've never danced need to—"

"Get up and dance?" Flash said, smirking. Since they'd started working together he loved repeating the name of the song. He said it at least ten times a day.

"Right," Twilight said.

"Let's get back to work, then," Rising Star said. "We still need to sync our song recording with the subliminal messages."

"Subliminal who?" asked Fluttershy.

"He means messages that affect you, even if you don't hear them or know they're there," Twilight explained. "And he's right. We don't have much time. I still haven't synced the light patterns to the music, and we have to set everything up in the gym tomorrow morning. The demonstration for the judges is first period."

"When do they announce the winner?" Sunset Shimmer asked.

"At the afterschool party," Ember said.

"We're on it," Blaze said. He was already sitting at the table with Rising Star, working on the music part of the machine. It was open so he could put the recorded message track into the mini computer inside. Twilight waved over Rainbow Dash and Fluttershy to help her with the lighting.

As everyone in the garage sprang into action, Twilight was more hopeful than she had been in days. This is what Principal Celestia meant when she'd said she wanted Crystal Prep and Canterlot High to come together. For once, Twilight wasn't paying attention to who was from which school, or whom she'd met before and whom she hadn't. Everyone was on the same team, focused on the same things, for the same goal.

She had to admit... that felt *wonderful*.

CHAPTER

13

Movin' and Groovin'

"The judges are coming!" Fluttershy said, peeking into the gym. Everyone inside started moving twice as fast as before, putting the finishing touches on their projects. Twilight arranged five chairs in front of their machine, which was resting on a stool they'd borrowed from the science wing. They'd tested it a dozen times, but never on someone who knew nothing about it. Would it actually work on Principal Cinch? Or Dean Cadance? Could it really inspire *anyone* get up and dance?

Blaze and Flash had decided to enter their rain cloud project after all, since Principal Celestia had allowed them to be part of both teams. Now they had a plexiglass box set up to show how rain was made from seawater. Foggy Blue, a shy Canterlot High sophomore, had one of the coolest projects. She and her partner, a Crystal Prep boy, made a robot dog that responded to voice commands. They could make it sit, beg, or roll over.

Twilight had spent the first ten minutes of setup playing with it.

"They're here!" Fluttershy said as she slipped inside the gym. Principal Celestia, Vice Principal Luna, Principal Cinch, and Dean Cadance were right behind her. They were each carrying a clipboard and pen. When they walked into the gym, everyone ran beside their projects.

"Wow," Principal Celestia said, taking in the different projects. "Thank you all for coming today and for all your hard work preparing. Just taking a quick glance around, I can already tell we're in for a real treat. Look at all these phenomenal displays."

There was a project on microwave

radiation and another on static electricity. A junior from Crystal Prep and a quiet freshman from Canterlot were eager to present their experiment on how time passes differently for people of different ages. Everyone stood next to their projects, waiting for the judges to come over. Twilight's team was the only group with more than two people in it, so they made a small arc around the machine, surrounding it.

The judges went to the far corner of the room first, looking at Blaze and Flash's project. Blaze started explaining how ocean water evaporated and stayed in the atmosphere. Then it formed into clouds and then raindrops. The judges nodded and smiled as Blaze did most of the talking.

"What do you think our chances are?" Pinkie Pie whispered to Twilight. "You think we could actually win?"

"I do," Twilight said. "If our Party Mood Modifier works on all four judges? That would be huge...."

"It will," Rising Star said. He took a deep breath and smiled. "After everything we did in the last three days, it has to."

After the judges finished up with Blaze and Flash, the two boys came over and joined Twilight's team. They had to wait for the judges to listen to the presentation on microwave radiation, but after that it was their turn.

"Come, please, sit," Rising Star said. He led Principal Celestia, Vice Principal Luna, Principal Cinch, and Dean Cadance to seats in front of the machine. "We are proud to present our project for the Canter-Crys science fair: the Party Mood Modificator."

Twilight Sparkle stepped forward. "Have you ever been to a school dance where everyone was sitting down? Where the dance floor was empty and it was kind of…boring?"

Principal Celestia nodded. "I have been to one or two of those over the years…."

"What if there were a way to liven up any party or event?" Sunset Shimmer asked. "If you could influence people in a big way, so before they knew it…they had to get up and dance?"

Principal Cinch shook her head. "Some people just don't like dancing," she muttered. "What's wrong with that?"

"But sometimes people don't like dancing because they're afraid they won't be good at it," Rising Star said. "Or they're afraid they'll embarrass themselves. With this machine, they won't have to worry about any of that. It frees you up to just—"

"Get up and dance?" Dean Cadance asked with a smile.

"Exactly," Flash said. "We've combined a music track with subliminal messages and a visual light pattern to influence crowds. Now, who here would say they *do not* like to dance?"

Principal Cinch raised her hand.

Vice Principal Luna just shrugged. "I don't usually dance at big events," she said. "I get nervous in front of people I don't know that well. It feels as if everyone is watching me."

"Then you're a perfect fit for this experiment," Sunset Shimmer said. "We've tried it on a few of our friends, but if it works here today, that'll prove this machine can be used in big crowds. Hundreds, maybe thousands of people dancing together. All because of us. But, of course, you should only give in to the beat if you want to."

"I'll believe it when I see it," Principal Cinch said.

Twilight nodded, and their entire team put on sunglasses so they wouldn't be affected by the light patterns. Then she switched the machine on. The Sonic Rainbooms' song blasted throughout the gym.

"Any party's not complete, until you rule the beat…"

At first they didn't notice anything different. The judges just sat in their chairs, staring at the light patterns the machine threw off. The rest of the kids in the gym barely paid any attention to them. They were tweaking their own projects, getting ready for the judges to finish up with Twilight and Rising Star so they could start their presentations.

"Oh no..." Fluttershy whispered. "It doesn't seem as if it's working. What if we messed something up?"

Twilight's stomach twisted into knots. Maybe she hadn't gotten the exact patterns right, or she'd picked the wrong shade of red for the lightbulbs. But hadn't Rarity felt something when Twilight had tried it out on her?

Just then Principal Celestia's shoulders began to shimmy. Dean Cadance started tapping her foot to the music. Even Principal Cinch cracked a smile. She wiggled in her seat, as if she might hop up at any moment and bust a move.

"Look!" Rarity pointed to two Crystal Prep girls in the corner of the gym. They had abandoned their projects and were dancing, spinning around and bumping their hips together. A few other teams joined them. Within seconds, the empty space in the center of the gym had become a dance floor. Even the judges got up to dance.

"Rock out, let your hair down," the recording sounded. *"We're gonna let loose and rule this town. We're gonna get up and dance! We gotta get up and dance!"*

Principal Cinch threw her hands up in the air, then dropped them down to the floor. When she finally stood, she started moving around the dance floor like a robot, swinging her arms out in different directions. Every few seconds she threw in a different dance move to mix it up.

"Are you watching this?" Fluttershy asked. "She's on fire!"

"If this machine can convince Cinch to dance," Twilight said, "it can get anyone to dance. Whoa."

Cinch did the "lawn mower," walking in circles and pretending she was cutting grass. Then she did the "running man" for a little while. Dean Cadance did it beside her, moving her fists around in little circles. It was a spontaneous dance party for the ages!

CHAPTER

14

Save a Dance

Twilight started to fade out the music, but it took a whole minute for the group to slowly stop dancing.

Vice Principal Luna cleared her throat and looked around. "Well, um, that was quite the song, girls," she said nervously. "I've never danced quite like that before."

"I was just…experimenting. That wasn't *dancing*.…I…uh…" Dean Cadance started unconvincingly.

Principal Cinch looked horrified. "That machine!" she cried, pointing to their project. "It *hypnotized* us!"

"No! It just put you in the exact right mood to dance," Twilight tried. "Brainwashing not included. And we've decided to keep our design secret, so it's never used for the wrong purposes."

"I can't believe it!" Vice Principal Luna said happily. She looked down at her arms and legs, as if they didn't belong to her. "That's amazing! Dancing really is so fun."

The judges grabbed their clipboards and scribbled down their scores. Then they moved on to the next project, even though they still kept talking about the Party Mood Modificator.

"Was I really doing the 'lawn mower'?" Principal Cinch asked Dean Cadance under her breath.

"I'm pretty sure we all were…" Dean Cadance replied. "You looked great, Principal."

As the judges sat down for Lotus's solo presentation on earthquakes, Twilight's team formed a group huddle.

"I think it couldn't have gone any better," Twilight said.

"Now we just have to wait," Rising Star added. "And I hate waiting."

"Let's meet back here after school for the party," Sunset Shimmer added. "I'm trying not to get my hopes up for space camp...but my hopes are up! That was awesome!"

As Rising Star and Sunset Shimmer packed up the machine, Flash came over to Twilight. They'd been so busy putting the finishing touches on their project, they'd barely gotten a chance to talk. After all that, Twilight wasn't even sure what to say.

"I think you did really well," Flash tried a little awkwardly. "Good job, Twilight."

"Thanks, but it was a team effort. I couldn't have done it without you, either," Twilight responded as she stared out thoughtfully into the gym. She watched

Lotus's presentation. Lotus had drawn a lot of diagrams of the earth's crust, and she was describing how it moved during earthquakes.

"About before," Flash started. "I never got a chance to tell you....I'm sorry about what I said. I didn't mean anything about you or the Friendship Games or anything. I just...I really thought Rising Star was doing something evil."

Twilight let out a deep breath. She'd forgiven Flash as soon as he'd walked into the science lab and tackled Rising Star. Now that she knew what he'd seen in the garage, she understood why he'd thought something really strange was going on. It all made sense, even if what he'd said had hurt her feelings.

"I know," Twilight said. "I know. It's okay."

"And I don't think about Mid-Sparkle, or whatever her name was, anymore. I never thought of you that way," he went on. "I think you're...perfect."

Twilight could feel the heat creep up her cheeks. She didn't dare look at Flash. Instead she kept watching Lotus's science fair presentation. "Thanks, Flash...."

He just shrugged. "No problem. I'll see you after school, at the party, right? Will you save a Get Up and Dance for me?"

"Stop saying it that way!" Twilight laughed.

Flash smiled at her, and this time she looked right back at him. Was she imagining it, or was he being super nice to her?

Like, maybe *too* nice? He didn't like her like *that*, did he?!

"See you later, Twilight," Flash said. Then he left, glancing over his shoulder one last time to smile at her.

CHAPTER 15

Who's Going to Space Camp?

"You all did tremendous work," Principal Celestia said. "The scores were very close, and it came down to only a few points difference."

All the students gathered around the

judges. The gym was packed with people. Teams could invite as many guests as they wanted, so the crowd was filled with friends and parents. They'd spent the afternoon eating pizza, drinking lemonade, and waiting for the judges to show up. Now that they had made their decision, Twilight was more nervous than ever.

"Do you think they'll send all of us to space camp, or just you and me?" Rising Star whispered. "I'd understand if they could only send the two of us, wouldn't you? Sending eleven people to Space Camp is a whole different story."

"I don't know, Rising Star," Twilight mumbled. She'd barely heard a word he'd said. She couldn't stop staring at the piece of paper in Principal Celestia's hands. Was it possible they'd won?

Principal Celestia, Vice Principal Luna, Principal Cinch, and Dean Cadance were all on the small stage they'd set up for the event. Principal Celestia cleared her throat. "Third place goes to Crystal Prep's Evening, who was partnered with Moonshadows from Canterlot High. We award this to them for their project on microwave radiation."

The two students went onto the stage and accepted the yellow ribbons Dean Cadance handed them. Principal Cinch just stood there, staring out into the audience with a stiff, forced smile.

"Second place goes to…" Principal Celestia looked out into the crowd.

"This is it," Pinkie Pie whispered, grabbing Twilight's hand. "If we're not second place, then we won. We won the whole thing—we had to have won."

"Rising Star from Crystal Prep and Twilight Sparkle of Canterlot High," continued Principal Celestia. "The leaders of Team Get Up and Dance, for their irresistible Party Mood Modifier."

The crowd clapped and cheered. Twilight had to remind herself to smile. She knew second place was still great, but she'd gotten her hopes up that maybe, just maybe, they'd won first. She and Rising Star took the stage and shook hands with all the judges, then accepted their red ribbons. Vice Principal Luna gave them a whole stack so everyone on their team could have their own.

"Oh man…" Rising Star muttered as they got off the stage. "I could've sworn we were getting first. Who was better than us?"

"And first place goes to Foggy Blue of Canterlot High and Hornet of Crystal Prep," Principal Celestia read off the paper. "Their project was Robot Dog, who we very much enjoyed meeting. Congratulations, Foggy Blue and Hornet— you'll be heading to space camp this summer!"

The crowd hooted even louder than before. Foggy Blue had brought her entire family to the science fair, and all three of her brothers were cheering at the top of their lungs. Twilight had to admit it—Robot Dog was one of the coolest science fair projects she'd ever seen. If they had to lose, she was glad it was to Foggy Blue.

"We tried our best," Fluttershy said, giving Twilight a big hug.

"We did," Twilight said. All her friends slowly made their way to the other side of the gym. The Sonic Rainbooms had promised a live performance of "Get Up and Dance," and they still hadn't finished setting up their instruments.

"Come on! A *robot dog*?" Rising Star muttered. He rolled his eyes and then set off for the snack table. Flash passed him on his way.

"I think I finally found one of Rising Star's flaws," Flash said, looking to Twilight. "He may be smart, handsome, charming, and kind…but he's also a sore loser."

"I think you're right." Twilight laughed.

The Sonic Rainbooms played their first few notes, testing the microphones. Sunset Shimmer waved for Flash and Twilight to join them for the song.

Twilight glanced at Flash. "Should we—"

"Get up and dance?" Flash asked. "Yeah, I think we should. You can skip being a backup singer this one time, right?"

Twilight felt as if her stomach were filled with butterflies. Was that Flash's way of asking her to dance? By asking her *not to* sing?

"Yeah..." she said. She turned to Sunset Shimmer and gave a hand signal telling her to go on without her. Then Rainbow Dash's voice counted them off. Soon the whole gym was filled with music.

She followed Flash out onto the dance floor. The two of them started the party, spinning and shimmying to the beat. He grabbed her hand and spun her around once. It was so fun she couldn't help but laugh.

"See!" Flash said over the music. "Sometimes the best dancing is done without any... *influence*."

He slid back and did a quick spin,

throwing his hands up in the air. He looked like a real pro. It made Twilight want to make up her own moves. It also made her very, very happy.

You're right, she thought, spinning beside Flash. *There's nothing better than this.*

Twilight Sparkle's Signature Style

Twilight Sparkle is the queen of **geek chic** or, as she likes to call it, smart chic. And what exactly is **geek chic**? Quite simply, it is transforming traditionally **"geeky"** pieces into hip, smart, and totally **chic** fashion statements.

It is time to embrace your *glasses*, your *loafers*, your *knee-high socks*, and your *necktie blouses* because these pieces have never been more stylish…and Twilight Sparkle shows the world how to wear them like a pro! Twilight Sparkle's statement-making glasses are her number-one accessory. Not only do they help her see, they also complete her look. They bring an extra dose of *personality and polish*, and, thanks to a few spare pairs, she can change them to fit her mood.

With an accessory game this strong, it could be easy for clothing to take a back seat, but Twilight Sparkle certainly doesn't let that happen. She actually takes her clothing to the next level. She has her favorite pieces, like a *bow-tie blouse* and *pleated skirt*, but she doesn't do basic. She mixes *patterns and prints*, and she doesn't shy away from color. Her clothing is *always classic*, so the way she puts it together is *definitely* smart chic.

Are You a Twilight Sparkle?

Let's talk about how you can recreate her look with some key pieces.

Cool-Girl Glasses

So many of us need some vision assistance, and there has never been a better time to make a statement with your specs. There are so many frames out there to choose. Twilight Sparkle's bold, black frames are certainly a standout, but plain frames are only beginning. **Glasses can be as unique as you are!**

There are so many websites and optical stores that will help you find the perfect pair based your face shape, needs, and price point. The sky is the limit! And if you don't happen to need real help with your vision, there are also lots of options with clear non-prescription lenses so you can still rock the glasses without the enhancements.

Neat Neckwear

Neckwear is not just for the guys. Sure, it's a trend inspired by menswear, but neckwear on the girls can be just as cool and even ultra feminine. When wearing

Shutterstock.com/Gordana Sermek

a necktie blouse or other neckwear, keep a few things in mind: The rest of your accessories should be relatively simple. You don't need fussy jewelry or other things competing. *Tuck in your shirt!* This look shines when it's paired with a skirt, pants, or jeans and then tucked in for a polished finish. Finally, don't be afraid to *layer it up*. Throw on a sweater or a blazer, or wear the blouse under an open-necked dress to complete your look.

Loafers and Lace-ups

When Twilight Sparkle reaches for a pair of shoes, they should be practical and fashionable—just like she is. Loafers and socks? Yes, please! Lace-up booties? Awesome! Wedge heels? For sure! Her shoes strike the perfect balance between style and function.

Miniskirt Staple

The miniskirt is one of Twilight Sparkle's most versatile pieces. It is the perfect balance of girlish whimsy and ladylike sophistication. It is not too short and never too tight. She loves a skirt with color and pattern, and it pairs perfectly with a cute sock-and-loafer combo. This is her ultimate wardrobe staple.

Style Twilight Sparkle!
Draw her a new outfit!

Twilight Sparkle loves her glasses. What is your number-one accessory and why?

Design a new pair of glasses for Twilight Sparkle!

Can you create three outfits for Twilight Sparkle using these tops and bottoms?

What would be Twilight Sparkle's biggest fashion Dos and Don'ts?

DOs

DON'Ts

Time to go to the mall! Fill out your Twilight Sparkle—inspired shopping list!

-
-
-
-
-
-
-
-

Can you spot which tops Twilight Sparkle has in her wardrobe?

About the Stylist

Laura Schuffman is a My Little Pony: Equestria Girls stylist. When she's not dressing Canterlot High's coolest friends, she also serves as a fashion stylist for a network television program. Her work has been featured in countless publications, magazine covers, advertising campaigns, and commercials around the world!